Little Dinosaur

Mike Thaler

Illustrated by Paige Miglio

Henry Holt and Company • New York

Henry Holt and Company, LLC, *Publishers since 1866*
115 West 18th Street, New York, New York 10011

Henry Holt is a registered trademark of Henry Holt and Company, LLC
Text copyright © 2001 by Mike Thaler
Illustrations copyright © 2001 by Paige Miglio
Published in Canada by Fitzhenry & Whiteside Ltd.,
195 Allstate Parkway, Markham, Ontario L3R 4T8.

Library of Congress Cataloging-in-Publication Data
Thaler, Mike. Little Dinosaur / by Mike Thaler; illustrations by Paige Miglio.
Summary: Little Dinosaur enjoys playing with blocks, wearing new clothes,
learning the alphabet, and being kind to ants. [1. Dinosaurs—Fiction.]
I. Miglio, Paige, ill. II. Title. PZ7.T3 Li 2001 [E]—dc21 00-47133
ISBN 0-8050-6213-0 / First Edition—2001 / Designed by Donna Mark
Printed in the United States of America on acid-free paper. ∞

The artist used watercolor and water-soluble color pencil on Lana 140-pound
cold-pressed paper to create the illustrations for this book.

10 9 8 7 6 5 4 3 2 1

The Caps

Little Dinosaur
had two caps.
He had a daytime cap.
He had a nighttime cap.
He wore his daytime cap
all day.

Then when he went to sleep,
he put on his nighttime cap.
He loved both his caps.
His daytime cap
was full of sunshine.
His nighttime cap
was full of dreams.

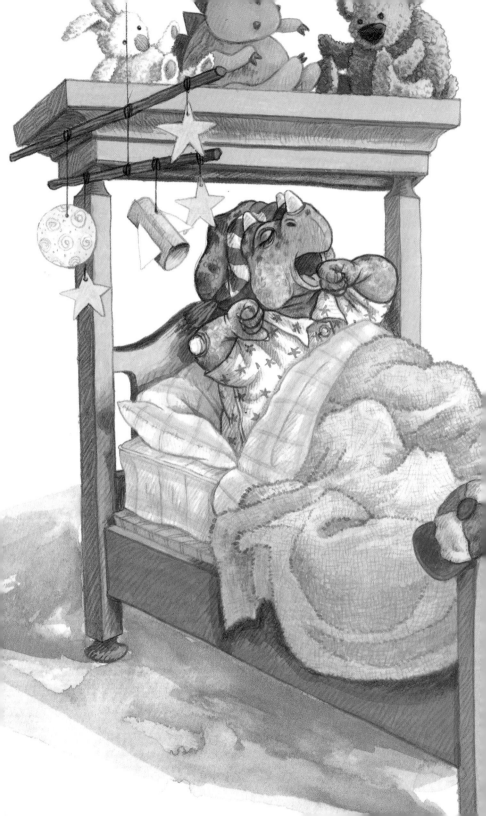

Morning

Little Dinosaur
woke up
when his eyes woke up.

He jumped
out of bed
into brand-new pants.

He hopped into brand-new shoes.
He put on
a brand-new shirt,

and stepped outside
into
a brand-new
day!

The Picture

Little Dinosaur painted a picture.
He made a purple tree
with orange leaves.
He made a yellow sky
with a blue sun.
He painted white sheep
in the sky.

Little Dinosaur laughed.
"Sheep can't fly," he said.

So he turned their feet
into raindrops,
and made them
a flock of clouds.

The Blocks

Little Dinosaur had four blocks.

When he put them in line,
they were a train.

When he put them on top of
one another, they were a rocket.
When he put them together
in a square, they were a house.

Some days Little Dinosaur
rode the train
to the rocket, and blasted off
for the moon.

He spent the day
on the moon,
then flew back to Earth,
and took the train
home.

Some days he just rode the train
all around the world.

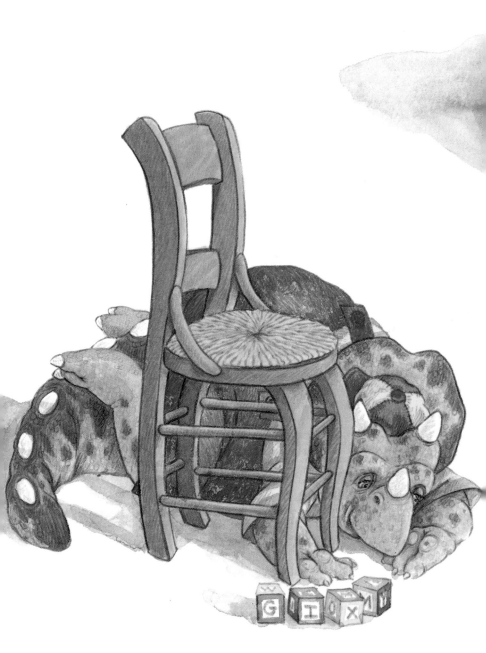

And some days
he just
stayed
home.

The Alphabet

Little Dinosaur learned to print
the alphabet.
He liked to make all the letters,
but some were his favorites.
He liked the **M**,
because it looked like mountains.

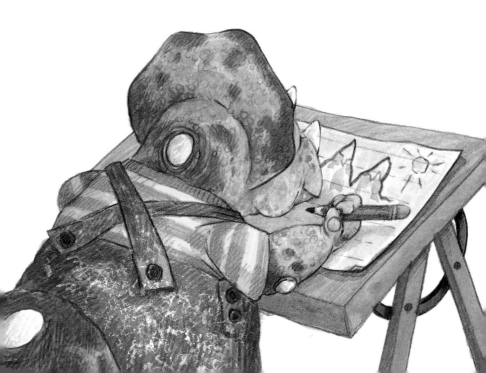

He liked the **S**,
because it was a snake.
He liked the **O**,
because it was fun trying to make
the ends meet.

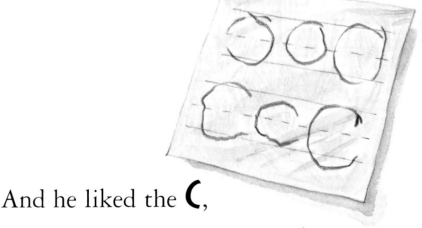

And he liked the **C**,
because he didn't have to make
the ends meet.

But best of all he liked
the **U**.
It made him the happiest.
It was the letter
with the biggest
smile.

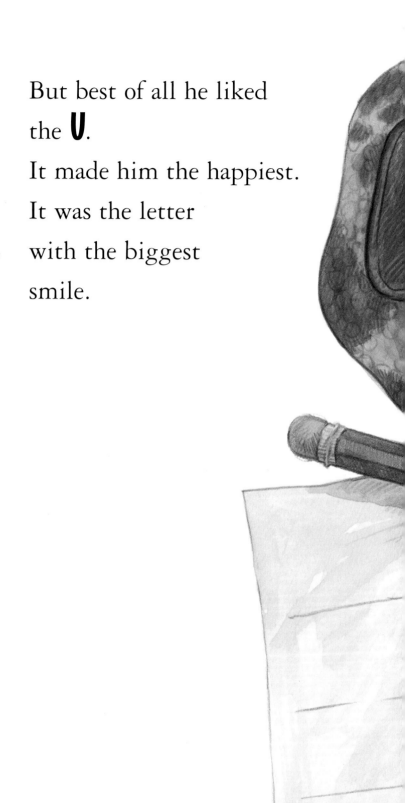

Ants

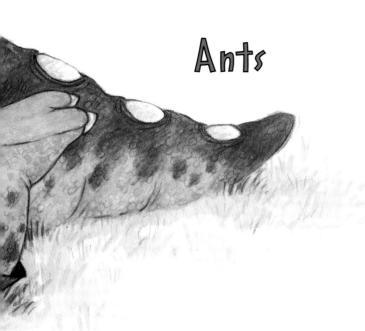

Little Dinosaur was bigger
than ants.
So he was very careful
not to step on any.
But he was so much bigger,
he didn't mind
if any
stepped on him.

The Kite

Little Dinosaur loved
to fly his kite.
He held tight
to the end of the string.
He ran along the ground.
The kite rose
high in the air.
The kite fished
for clouds.

The kite danced
in the sky.
Little Dinosaur danced
on the ground.
Sometimes he wished
it were the other way
around.

The Rainbow

Little Dinosaur saw a rainbow
that spread across the sky.
He could see many colors:
red, orange, yellow,
green, blue, purple.

"Someone must have big crayons,"
he told his mom,
as he colored a little rainbow
on a little
piece of paper.

The Trick

Little Dinosaur learned
a card trick.
He had one card.
He held it out to his mom.
"Pick a card," he said.
She picked the card.
Little Dinosaur thought real hard,
he said the magic words,
then he guessed the card.
"Very good!" said his mom.

He did the trick
with his dad.
"Very good," said his dad.
He did the trick
with his sister.
"That's not a trick,"
said his sister.
"You only have one card."
"I'm just starting out,"
said Little Dinosaur.
"When I get really good,
I'll get more cards."

The Book

Little Dinosaur turned on the TV.
It was broken.

Little Dinosaur turned
on the computer.
It was broken.

Little Dinosaur turned on the radio.
It was broken too.

Little Dinosaur
began to cry.
His sister
handed him a book.
He opened it.
He read it.
He looked at the pictures.
It wasn't broken.
It worked fine!

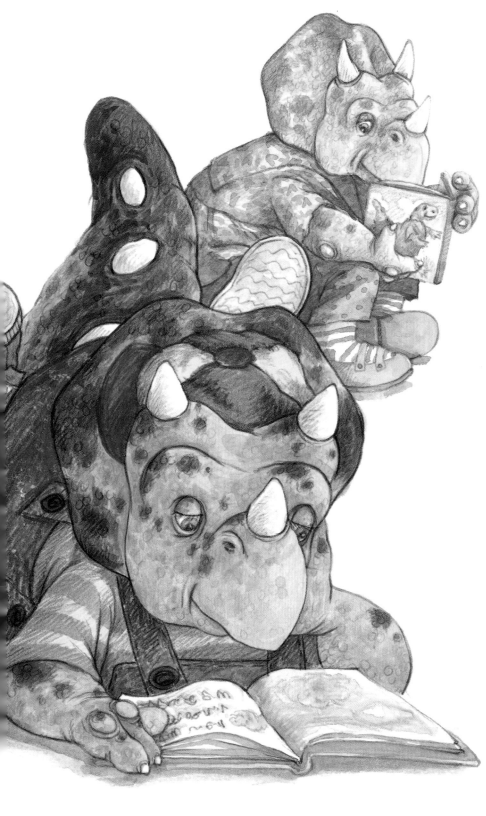

The Tub

When Little Dinosaur took a bath
he had lots of toys.

He had a battleship.

He had an alligator.

He had a duck.

He would have great sea battles
between them.
Sometimes the battleship
would sink the alligator.
Sometimes the alligator
would eat the battleship.

But most of the time the duck
would scold them both,
and they would make up
and have a parade
around
the pond.

Buttons

Little Dinosaur
hated to button
his pajamas.
But every night
he had to.
There were five buttons
and five buttonholes.

Sometimes
he would start at the top
and button down.

Sometimes
he would start at the bottom
and button up.

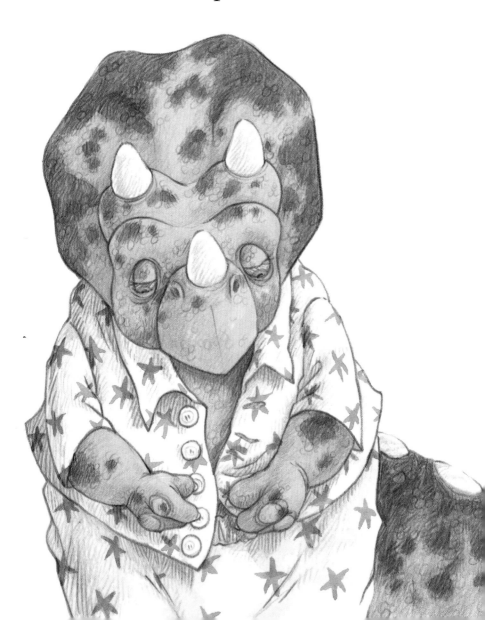

He would carefully put each button
into a buttonhole.
But when he was done,
he would have an extra button
at one end
and an extra buttonhole
at the other.
That meant he would have to
unbutton every button, and then
button them all over again.
This is why Little Dinosaur
hated to button his pajamas
every night.

The All-Day Sucker

Little Dinosaur
got an all-day sucker.
He didn't unwrap it
in the morning.

He didn't unwrap it
in the afternoon.

He didn't unwrap it
at night.

Then right before
he went to sleep,
he unwrapped it.
He put the whole sucker
in his mouth.

With one crunch
and one munch,
he ate it.
Little Dinosaur smiled.
What a good sucker it was.
It tasted great . . .

. . . and it had lasted
all day!

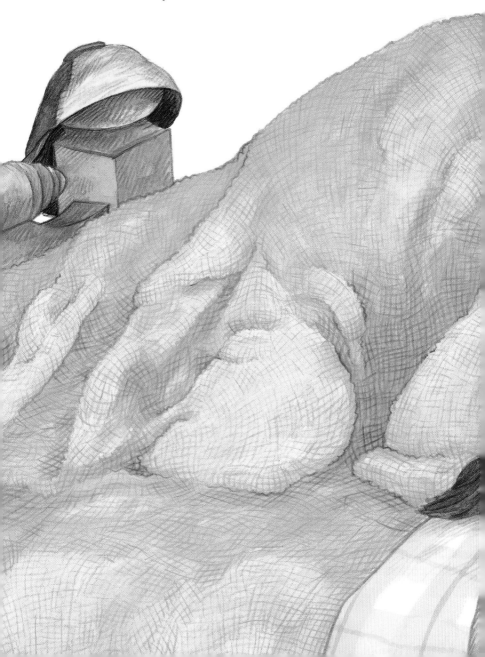